Is That My Watson?

Written by Andrew Murray
Illustrated by Deakin Brook

First edition published in 2013

Paperback ISBN 9781780925264
ePub ISBN 9781780925271
PDF ISBN 9781780925288

Published in the UK by MX Publishing
335 Princess Park Manor, Royal Drive,
London, N11 3GX

www.mxpublishing.com

At Reichenbach Falls
by the thundering foams
We fought, Moriarty and I,
Sherlock Holmes...

In that desperate battle
I learned a good tip:
If you fight on a ledge
then you'd better not slip...

As I lay bruised and broken,
I hoped and I prayed
That MY Doctor Watson
would come to my aid…

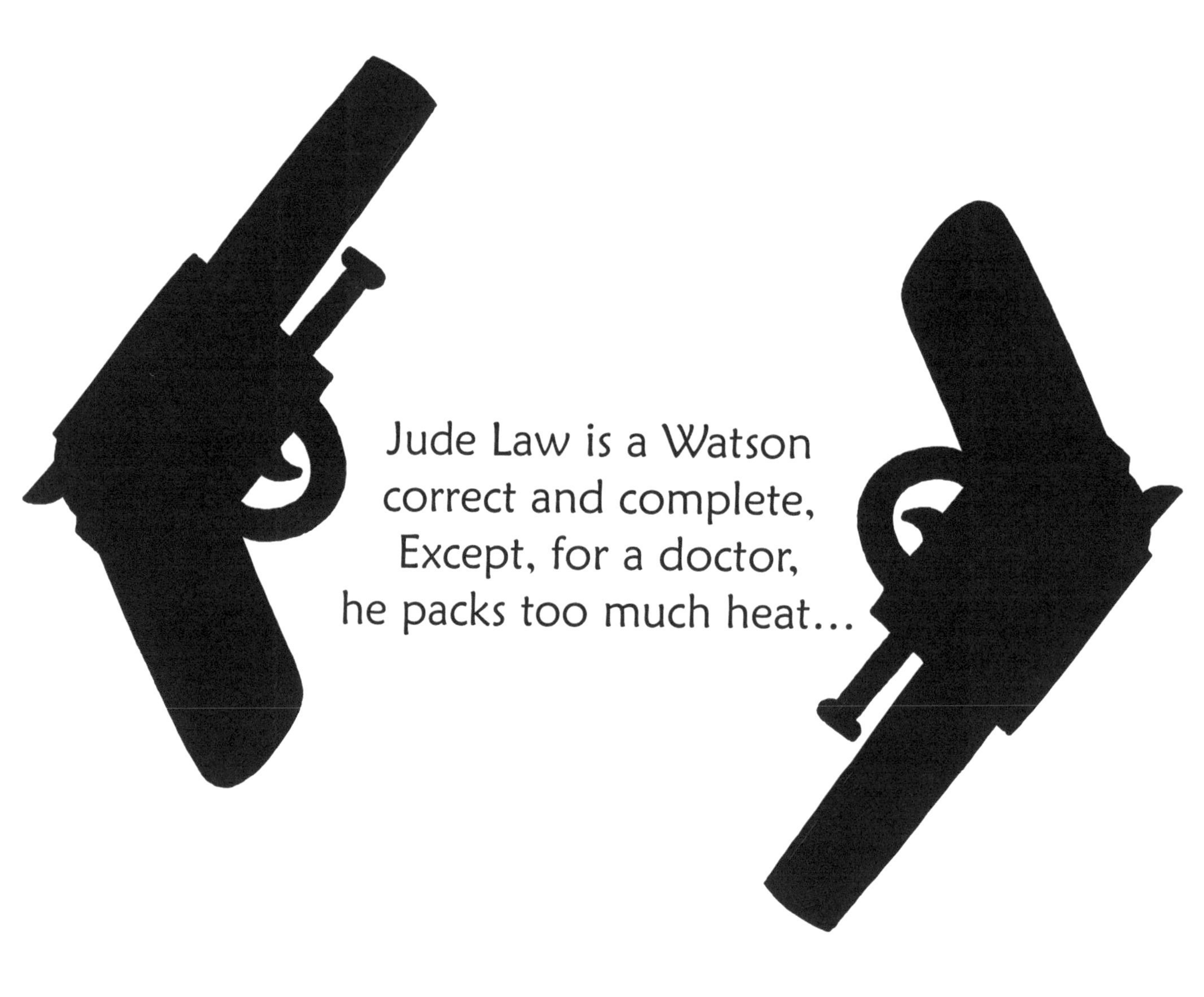

Jude Law is a Watson
correct and complete,
Except, for a doctor,
he packs too much heat…

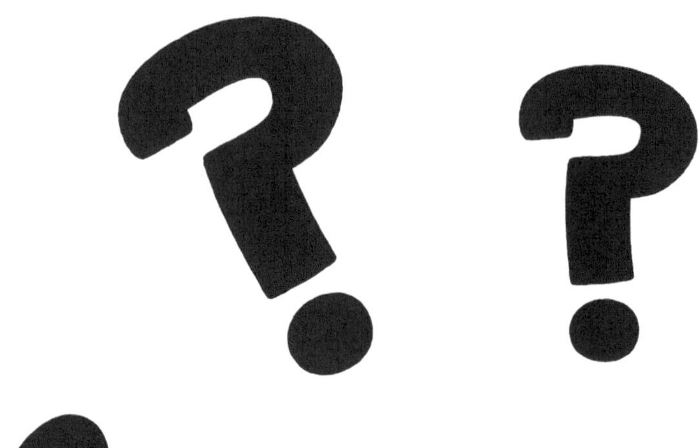

And poor Nigel Bruce,
what a bumbling clot -
If he is my doctor,
what chance have I got?

That nice Edward Hardwicke
does all that I ask,
But he looks like a man
in a teddy-bear mask…

This fellow L. Liu
is disturbingly pretty,
But learned all his knowledge
in quite the wrong city...

NY MAP

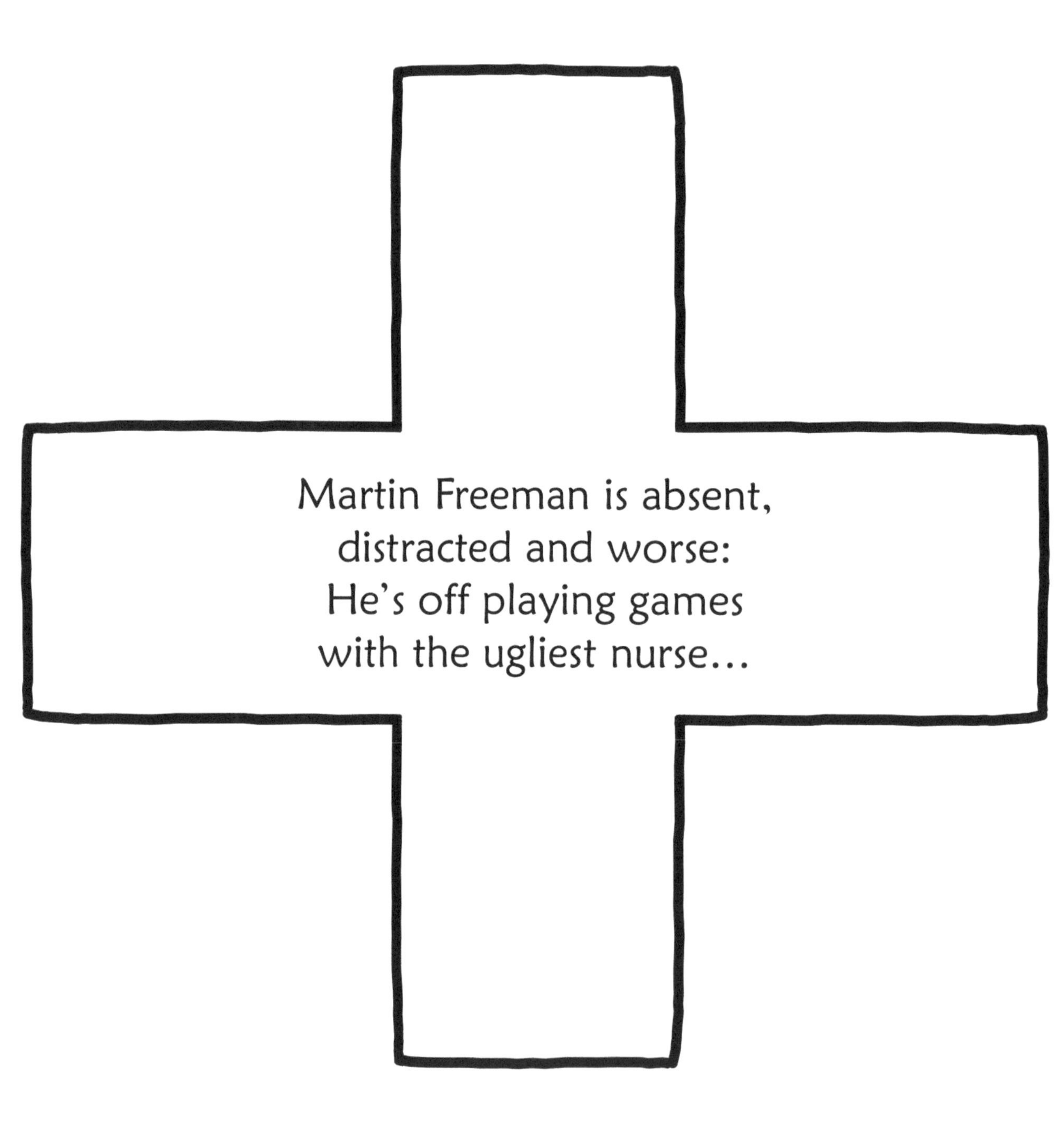
Martin Freeman is absent,
distracted and worse:
He's off playing games
with the ugliest nurse...

In the surgical theatre,
I fear for my life:
Which Watson is putting me
under the knife?...

Hullo! Now I know
that I'm going to be fine -
For this is my Watson,
this Watson is MINE!

This Watson is perfect for me,
it is true…
But who is the Watson
who's perfect for YOU?

www.ingramcontent.com/pod-product-compliance
Ingram Content Group UK Ltd.
Pitfield, Milton Keynes, MK11 3LW, UK
UKHW060116300726
14090UKWH00002B/215
9781780925264